Lulu's Hat

Susan Meddaugh

Houghton Mifflin Company Boston 2002

Walter Lorraine Books

Walter Lorraine (wL) Books

www.houghtonmifflinbooks.com

Library of Congress Cataloging-in-Publication Data

Meddaugh, Susan.
    Lulu's hat / Susan Meddaugh.
      p. cm.
    Summary: Although she sometimes fails to pull a rabbit out of her hat, Lulu the magician delights audiences with her unpredictable magic.
    ISBN 0-618-15277-6
      [1. Magicians—Fiction] I. Title.
PZ7.M51273 Le 2002
[E]—dc21

                                              2001016787

Printed in the United States
LBM 10 9 8 7 6 5 4 3 2 1

Lulu's Hat

1

An Unusual Talent

Everybody knew Lulu could never be the one. But that summer it was Lulu's turn. Hoping to discover the next magician in the family, each summer Uncle Jerry picked a different nephew or niece to assist him in his Traveling Magic Show. Lulu's Uncle Jerry was the magician of his generation. The chosen one. For in True Magic Families, only one member of each generation was born with the magician's touch. Real magic. It was a genetic quirk that no one could explain. Either you had it or you didn't.

Lulu's Great-Grandfather Marcus had it. He was Marko the Magnificent. Grandmother Izzy performed as The Invisible Isabel, and Uncle Jerry was simply Jerry the Great. Of course every child in the youngest generation dreamed about being the magician, but so far no one seemed to have the gift. Lulu was the only child who didn't think about it.

Lulu was a twelve-year-old girl who would not stand out in a crowd of other twelve-year-old girls. Unless of course you noticed her eyes. Lulu's eyes were such a pale shade of blue that they looked almost like water. But her eyes were not the problem. What made it impossible for Lulu to be the one was her genes. Lulu was adopted.

This was no secret. Lulu's parents had often told her how Uncle Jerry had discovered her during a performance in Atlantic City. "Abandoned backstage," they said. "You were just a tiny girl, holding on tight to a locket. All we could ever find out about you was your name. You kept repeating 'Lulu get lost.'"

Lulu still wore the locket, but if she had hoped to find a picture in it, some clue to her past, she was disappointed. The locket was impossible to open. What she, and all her relatives, did know was that Lulu had not been born into this True Magic Family. Therefore the genetic gift that made magic possible was not hers, and nothing could change that.

Still, Lulu wanted to have her summer as Uncle Jerry's assistant. She wanted to be a part of the Traveling Magic Show and see the world beyond Upper Parkington, New Jersey.

Her cousins were not very understanding. One cousin voiced what the others were thinking.

"It will just be a wasted summer," he said. "Why not take a cousin who has a chance?"

But Uncle Jerry was a kind and patient man. He knew the next magician would be revealed in time. And no summer could ever be called wasted when there was magic to be performed.

2

Lulu's Hat

Before they left Upper Parkington, Jerry told Lulu what she was expected to do as his assistant. He explained how the tricks worked and what her part would be in each one. "And," he said, "if you want to, you can do a few simple card tricks yourself to warm up the audience."

He showed Lulu how to do the tricks. Lulu was all thumbs.

"That's all right," her uncle said. "I'm the magician, not you." As if she needed a reminder.

Jerry had a trunk full of costumes worn by his previous assistants. Lulu tried on one outfit after another.

"No," she said.

"Not a chance," she said.

"HA HA!" she laughed.

Lulu dug deep into the old trunk. Her fingers found something flat and round. As she pulled it out, it suddenly snapped open, and Lulu was holding a shiny black top hat, just like her uncle's.

She put it on her head.

"I like this," she said.

An unusual choice, thought Jerry.

"That hat's been tucked in there for years," he told Lulu. He tried to remember where he'd picked it up. "I think you're the first assistant to actually wear it."

"Then it must be meant for me," said Lulu.

On the first day of summer vacation Uncle Jerry and Lulu packed the truck and said goodbye to the family. Lulu prepared to be sawed in half, to climb the magic rope, and to bring her uncle any items he might need during the act.

Their first stop was Mount Baldy, Pennsylvania. Lulu helped her uncle set up for the performance, then went off to get ready.

Although it was exciting to be in the show, a part of Lulu was disappointed when she thought about the card tricks her uncle had shown her.

"I should be able to do those tricks," she said to herself, "even if I'm not a magician."

After she had dressed, Lulu stood in front of the mirror. She

looked good, she thought. It was the hat that made the difference. Without it she looked like the same old Lulu. But when she put the hat on her head, she looked like a girl who could certainly do a simple card trick. Her fingers tingled as she picked up the deck of cards, and this time she knew exactly how to work the trick. A single card disappeared in a snap of the fingers, then reappeared in her other hand.

"I did it!" said Lulu.

She tried the other tricks that her uncle had shown her. Her fingers seemed to have a life of their own. She only had to want to do the trick and it was done.

It's the hat, thought Lulu, looking in the mirror. It must be magic. And as she had grown up in a True Magic Family, she did not find this entirely surprising.

Pocketing the deck of cards, she went off to find her uncle.

"I can do the card tricks now," she said.

Lulu was thrilled to open the show for her uncle. She asked members of the audience to pick cards and hold them behind their backs. Then she identified each hidden card. She was always right. She made cards disappear. Then she made them reappear, snatching them right out of thin air. It hardly mattered to Lulu that the audience wasn't paying much attention. They were waiting for Jerry the Great.

When Lulu left the stage, Jerry appeared in a dazzling

explosion of smoke and light. Lulu began to observe how he did each trick, and after every show she secretly practiced doing them. Lulu always wore her hat.

With the hat, she could do Jerry's tricks, all except one. She could not pull a rabbit out of the hat. She finally asked her uncle how he did it.

"The rabbit trick is a tradition," said Jerry. "You say the magic words. *Zatza Lepus Wagra Doozie.* You put your hand in the hat. You pull out a rabbit."

"I say the magic words. *Zatza Lepus Wagra Doozie.* I put my hand in the hat. I pull out a . . . fish!" said Lulu.

Uncle Jerry was astonished.

"Do that again," he said.

"*Zatza Lepus Wagra Doozie.* I put my hand in the hat. I pull out a . . . frog!" said Lulu.

"How did you do that?" asked Jerry.

"It's the hat," said Lulu. "I can do most of your tricks," she told him, "but the hat won't let me do this one."

Jerry looked at his niece with new interest.

"Show me what else you can do," he said, and Lulu performed all the tricks she had been practicing.

Jerry couldn't believe what he was seeing.

She can't be the one, he thought. *It's impossible!* To cover his confusion, he snapped at Lulu.

"You have to control a magic trick," he told her. "If you ask your hat for a rabbit, you should get a rabbit. Besides," he warned, "uncontrolled magic can be dangerous."

Lulu tried again. "*Zatza Lepus Wagra Doozie.* I put my hand in the hat. I pull out a . . . DANGEROUS banana!"

Jerry said, "Just keep the hat on your head."

Lulu never saw the faded card that had fallen from the lining of the hat.

Langston Caste
Now the magic begins

3

Lulu's Big Chance

Several weeks later, Jerry the Great came down with a not-so-great stomachache. He had made too many pancakes disappear from his breakfast plate.

"How can we call off the show?" he groaned. "It's the Fourth of July!"

"I can do the act," said Lulu.

Jerry studied his niece. She certainly could do the tricks. He still couldn't remember where he had picked up the hat, which he believed was indeed magic. Jerry was glad that Lulu had found it. He knew that the hat was helping her get over any disappointment she might have felt, not having the possibility of magic herself.

"Go ahead," said Jerry. "Do the act. But don't try anything you can't control."

When Lulu went on stage that day she did most of Jerry's tricks, and she did them perfectly. Coins disappeared into thin air and scarves turned into doves. She finished with the Magic Chicken Trick and the crowd applauded.

Lulu was feeling confident. So confident that she couldn't resist trying the hat trick.

This time I will control the magic, she thought, and she took the hat from her head.

"Ladies and Gentlemen," said Lulu. "I shall now pull a rabbit from this absolutely empty hat."

She concentrated on the magic words, and then said them with great feeling. *"Zatza Lepus Wagra Doozie!"* She reached into the hat.

Please, she thought, *let this really be a rabbit.*

"Yes!" said Lulu, pulling out her very first rabbit.

Then she took another look at the hat.

Uh oh! thought Lulu, as rabbit after rabbit hopped from the hat. They jumped from the stage into the audience. Rabbits were everywhere and they just kept coming. Parents were shouting. Children were laughing. And a small dog was racing around the tent, barking and chasing the rabbits.

"How do I stop this?" Lulu gasped. "Uncle Jerry will be furious!" But she couldn't help noticing that the children were having a wonderful time.

The dog was having a good time too. He was so fast he seemed to be everywhere. He chased the rabbits to the right. He chased them to the left. He chased them round and round in circles until the runaway bunnies could barely hop. In one great desperate effort to escape the little dog, they all ran straight toward Lulu.

They want to get back in the hat! she thought.

"Eizood Argaw Supel Aztaz!" said Lulu, reversing the spell.

She held out her hat and watched as every last rabbit hopped into it. Before she could stop him, the little dog disappeared into the hat as well.

After all the commotion, the tent was suddenly quiet. Then the audience began to clap. They laughed and stomped their feet.

"Great trick!" they shouted. "Bravo!"

They had never seen anything quite like it. They continued to clap, but Lulu barely heard them. She was thinking about the dog. As the crowd left the tent, Lulu stared into her hat.

Poor dog, she thought. *Lost in Deep Magic Space. I've got to get him back before his owner comes looking for him.*

Lulu found her uncle's *Handbook to Magic Tricks* and

turned to the chapter on lost objects. What words would make the dog reappear?

"Shazza Bowzer Googly Nowzer!" she said.

"Misin Nipso Puppy Yakie!" she said.

All sorts of things appeared. A sock. A glove. A pair of eye glasses. But no little dog.

Lulu flopped down on the edge of the stage.

"What's the matter?" asked a little boy.

"I've lost a dog," said Lulu.

"Have you looked everywhere?" asked the boy.

"He's not that kind of lost," Lulu explained. "I can't just say 'Here Boy!'"

No sooner were the words out of her mouth when Lulu heard a bark.

"Great trick!" said the boy.

The traveler to Deep Magic Space was back.

4

Lost Dog

Now that the little dog had come back from Deep Magic Space, Lulu assumed he would find his way home. He didn't. He sat next to the Magic Chicken cage while Lulu organized equipment for the next show. After supper he was waiting for her, and he was still with her when she was ready for bed.

"Tomorrow we will find your home," Lulu told him.

She was almost asleep when she felt a thump. The little dog had leaped onto the bed. He curled up beside her.

Lulu's family had owned lots of rabbits, a few doves, and chickens, but never a dog.

"If you were my dog . . ." she whispered. She put her arm around him and they both fell asleep.

The next day Lulu visited the police station, the dog pound, the local veterinarian's office, and the pet store. But by showtime she had not connected the little dog with his owner. Nor was she able to find his home the following day. There was only one solution. When Lulu and Uncle Jerry moved on to the next town, there was another member in the troupe.

5

Hereboy

By the time Jerry's Traveling Magic Show got to Gooseberry, Ohio, people had begun to hear about Lulu's hat. They lined up around the tent for tickets to the show. They applauded Jerry's perfect magic tricks, but then they wanted to see the hat. They were not disappointed.

If Jerry was still worried about uncontrolled magic, he didn't mention it again. The unpredictable hat was drawing larger and larger crowds.

Jerry discovered that people liked surprises, which was lucky because it wasn't always rabbits that came out of the hat. Sometimes it was mice. Or ferrets. Or giant cane toads.

Nobody claimed the little dog, and that was lucky too,

because no matter what came out of Lulu's hat, the dog could always round it up.

But for Lulu, it was better than lucky. She had found a friend. She named him Hereboy and wherever Hereboy went — into Deep Magic Space or out behind a tree — he always came back when Lulu said the magic words "Here Boy!"

6

Trouble

It was a hot day in late July when Jerry, Lulu, and Hereboy pulled into Shallow Pond, Indiana, where they joined a local carnival. Among the people who came to see them perform their magic was a boy who enjoyed a different kind of trick. His name was Earl Zopton. He had already short-sheeted his sister's bed and prepared ten water balloons to throw out his bedroom window when the moment was right. At the fairground Earl had loosened the tops on all the mustard and ketchup bottles at the food stands. His jaw ached from chewing forty pieces of Palooka bubble gum, but he smiled as he dropped the individual sticky blobs all over the ground for people to step on.

Earl wandered into the tent as Lulu did her hat trick.

Boy! thought Earl. *What I could do with that hat!*

Earl Zopton decided to see the show again.

The next day Earl was in the front row. He popped his bubble gum and daydreamed throughout Jerry the Great's performance. But when Lulu's act came on, he paid attention. When she took the hat off her head Earl leaned forward to hear the words she spoke.

"Zatza Lepus Wagra Doozie!" said Lulu.

On that night dozens of cats jumped out of the hat. Hereboy

particularly enjoyed chasing cats. Round and round they went as the children shrieked with laughter and the adults clapped their hands. As usual, Hereboy finally chased all the cats back into the hat. As usual, he disappeared into the hat as well. And, as usual, Lulu said the magic words. "Here Boy!" she called.

But this time Hereboy didn't come back.

7

Where's Hereboy?

It didn't matter to the audience. They applauded anyway.

Of course Earl Zopton didn't care. It wasn't his dog. He was wondering how he could get his hands on the hat.

But Lulu was worried.

"Here Boy!" she called. She looked deep into the bottomless hat. For the first time she wondered what it was like in Deep Magic Space. She wished she could see it.

"Here Boy!" she called again. *Something is definitely wrong,* she thought. *Hereboy always comes back.* She continued to say the magic words until the moon was high in the sky. Then she made a decision.

Lulu left her uncle a note, telling him she'd be back in time

for the next performance. She hoped she was telling the truth.

Then she found a secluded spot in the woods behind the tent. Before most people had eaten breakfast, Lulu said the magic words, stepped into her hat, and disappeared.

8

Earl Finds the Hat

If Earl Zopton hadn't been sneaking around trying to find a way to get into the tent, he never would have seen the hat.

It's fate, he thought. Without further consideration of right or wrong, Earl grabbed it and ran home. He sat on his bed with the hat in his lap, contemplating the possibilities.

I'll get my sister first, he thought.

Zoe Zopton's room was right next to Earl's. It was, at the moment, empty, but it wouldn't be for long, thought Earl. He planned to fill it up. Frogs, he thought. Or maybe snakes. It didn't matter. Earl would say the magic words and let the hat produce its multitude. Then Earl would close Zoe's door, go back to his room, and wait for the screaming to start. That was the plan.

Earl stood in the doorway of Zoe's room, ready for a fast getaway.

"Watza Leafy Waggin Doogie!" he said. With a big grin on his face, he held out the hat.

Nothing happened.

When he heard his sister's voice on the stairs, Earl was forced to make a quick retreat to his own messy room.

"What were those words?" he whined. *"Zatza Leopard Whatta Poodle,"* he said. *"Thatza Leapin Poogie Doogie,"* he said. *"Whatza Fatso Juicy Doozie! Zatza Lepus Wagra Doozie!* PHOOEY PHOOEY PHOOEY PHOOEY!" he yelled and threw the hat across the room. He lay back on his

bed and reached into an open box of cookies to soften his dis-appointment.

But something was happening in the hat, although it wasn't immediately obvious. Earl had accidentally come up with exactly the right magic words. As he fell into a light snooze, cookie crumbs falling onto his pillow, Earl was about to get what he deserved.

Ants. Millions of them.

9

Lulu in Deep Magic Space

Lulu's first impression of Deep Magic Space was no impression at all. But as she looked, objects began to appear. A green tree. A gray rock. *Like magic, of course!* thought Lulu.

"Here Boy!" she called. But there was no sign of the dog, and no clue as to which direction he might have gone.

Lulu was wondering what to do when she heard a voice.

"Help!" someone cried.

Lulu followed the cries until she came to a large box with feet sticking out of it. The feet were wiggling.

But the voice came from a second box. To be exact, it came from the mouth of half of a beautiful lady.

"Help me!" said the lady.

"Oh, I know this trick," said Lulu. She pushed the boxes together and removed the square metal slabs between them.

When the lady lifted the lid and stepped out, she seemed surprised and excited to see Lulu.

"Where did you come from?" she asked.

"Indiana," said Lulu.

"Do you know how to get back?" asked the lady.

"I hadn't really thought about that," Lulu admitted.

"Oh," said the lady. "Too bad. I had hoped . . . oh well. It will be nice to have another person here."

10

Ants in Earl's Pants

Earl Zopton woke up with a start. He had the strangest feeling that his clothes were alive. He looked down and . . .

"EEEEEEK!" shrieked Earl. "EEEEEEEEEEEK!"

His mother came running up the stairs, taking two at a time.

"Ants!" she bellowed. "Earl Zopton, have you been eating cookies in bed again?"

Earl's mother was not to be trifled with. Built like a rhinoceros, with the strength to match, she grabbed Earl by the ear and hauled him downstairs. Outside she turned the hose on him at full force. When all the ants were washed away, she got out her Bug Blaster and sprayed Earl's room until it looked like a foggy day.

"It was the hat," whined Earl. "The hat did it."

"The hat?" said his mother, in a dangerously low and barely controlled voice. "This hat?"

Earl could tell she didn't believe him for a minute.

She picked up the hat and hurled it through the open window. It sailed across the yard and landed in that very same shallow pond for which the town was named. It floated for a while, but gradually it began to sink.

11

Losing Ground in Deep Magic Space

My name is Laura Lee Stump," said the lady. "I worked for Langston Caste. I was his assistant . . . until he disappeared."

"Did Langston Caste leave you in the box?" asked Lulu.

"Oh, no," said Laura Lee. "That was Junior. He talked me into letting him try one of Langston's tricks. Then he saw a little dog and he ran off after it."

"A dog!" said Lulu. "Which way did they go?"

"There's only one direction to go in Deep Magic Space," Laura Lee told her. "Deeper."

The pair started off toward a mountain that Lulu was sure hadn't been there before. Laura Lee seemed pleased to have someone to talk to.

"Langston Caste was a great magician," she told Lulu. "It

was so exciting being his assistant. Deep Magic Space was his home, but we performed all over the world. He said he was always looking for new ideas."

Lulu was about to ask her how Langston Caste had disappeared when she noticed something strange.

"Does the ground feel funny to you?" she said. It was becoming spongy and moist.

They walked farther and the ground got wetter. Soon they were walking in water up to their ankles. They walked faster as the water rose up to their knees.

Then the water was rising very quickly.

Objects began to float by.

"There's my box!" Laura Lee shouted, and she grabbed on to it.

"Lulu!" she cried as she floated out of sight.

The water was over Lulu's head. What had once been solid ground was now a raging river, and Lulu was only one of many objects being swept along. She saw a crystal ball float up to the surface. A rabbit swam past. Lulu was frantically

trying to keep her head above water when a large box bobbed up beneath her. It lifted her above the water and carried her along with the current. There were two heavy straps wrapped around the box, and Lulu grabbed on to one.

Then she saw an incomprehensible and terrifying sight. Straight ahead there was nothing. Nothing at all. It looked as if Lulu was about to drop off the end of the earth. She closed her eyes and held on tight to the strap.

12

Earl Saves the Hat

As soon as Earl Zopton's mother left to go shopping, he went looking for the hat. He waded into the water and grabbed

it just before it sank below the surface. He poured out the water, but now the hat was thoroughly soaked. Earl was going to lay the hat in the sun to dry out when a better idea occurred to him.

13

Who's in the Box?

In Deep Magic Space, Lulu did not fall off the end of the earth. Instead, she felt a jarring bump as the box came to a stop. The water level had suddenly dropped, and the box had hit bottom.

"Ouch!" cried a voice inside the box.

Lulu jumped off into mud up to her ankles.

"Darn it!" said the voice again. Someone was moving around inside the box.

"Who's in there?" said Lulu.

"It's me. *Ben,*" said the voice. "Can you help?"

The box that had saved Lulu's life was actually an old trunk with an even older-looking lock. Lulu unbuckled the straps

first. She gave the lock a little tug and it fell open in her hand. When she lifted the lid, a young man stood up.

"Thank you," he said. "You must be a very great magician."

"Oh, no!" said Lulu, laughing. "I'm not a magician at all."

Then she noticed that he was handcuffed.

"Who did this to you?" said Lulu angrily.

Now Ben looked embarrassed.

"I did it to myself," he admitted. "I guess I still have a lot to learn. I was Langston Caste's apprentice, and I was practicing an escape trick. I had just locked myself into the trunk and put on the handcuffs when suddenly the box started to move . . . and I dropped the key."

Ben spotted the key in a corner of the trunk. He grabbed it and undid the handcuffs. Holding it up, he said, "This unlocks the secret escape panel too. Which reminds me: How did you open the lock? Only Langston Caste could do that without the key. He had real magic."

"You must not have closed it all the way," Lulu told him. "It just came open when I pulled on it."

Lulu was curious about Langston Caste.

"Laura Lee said he disappeared."

"That's true," said Ben. "He's been gone for over a year. Something terrible must have happened to him. He never would have left us here with no way to get out."

No way to get out? thought Lulu. It hadn't occurred to her that she wouldn't be able to trace her steps backward to the hat. Now she looked around and realized that after her wild ride on the river, she wasn't even sure which direction *was* back.

14

Earl Blows It Again

Earl Zopton was back in his sister's room. He put the dripping hat under the bonnet of her hair dryer and turned it on high. Never having used a hair dryer, Earl had no idea how long it would take to dry out the hat. Or how hot it could get.

This should take a while, he thought, and he went downstairs to make himself a peanut butter and banana sandwich. When Earl went back upstairs to retrieve the hat, the hair dryer had just begun to smoke.

15

Strange Weather

In Deep Magic Space, a dry hot wind was blowing.

"Is it always like this?" asked Lulu. "I mean, first it was wet, and now it's hot and windy."

"Only today," said Ben. "It's very weird."

The mud was drying out quickly, and Lulu realized that she could now walk on it.

"I'm looking for my dog," she told Ben. "I was going toward a mountain, but it doesn't seem to be there anymore."

"There's only one direction to go in Deep Magic Space," said the young man.

"I know," said Lulu. "Deeper."

Ben laughed. "Come on," he said. "We'll find your dog."

But as the wind grew hotter and stronger, the first thing they would have to find was shelter. In the distance a forest appeared. Surely it would be cooler there.

Walking toward the forest Lulu could feel the heat right through her sneakers. She worried that the rubber soles would melt.

At last they stumbled into the forest, but there was no relief from the heat beneath these trees. How strange it was! This forest was dark as night, and yet it felt as hot as an August day on the Jersey shore. They had only walked for a few minutes when Lulu realized that Ben was no longer with her.

"Ben!" she shouted. But the trees muffled her voice, and there was no response.

Lulu's mouth was so dry that all she could think about was a cool glass of water. She remembered reading somewhere that sucking on a button would keep your mouth from drying out.

Did she have a button? Only on her pants. If she pulled the button off, her pants might fall down. What if Ben reappeared? She would die of embarrassment. Better to die of embarrassment than from the heat.

Then she remembered the locket. *Better not to die at all,* she thought.

Sucking on her locket, Lulu started walking. But in the darkness her foot caught on a root. Lulu fell hard to the ground, her teeth crunching down on the locket. She could tell immediately that the fall had broken it open, but it was so dark that she couldn't see what was inside. There would be time to study it later, she decided. If she ever got out of the forest.

16

Earl's Cool Idea

As smoke filled his sister's room, Earl turned off the hair dryer and snatched the hat.

"YEEOUCH!" he cried, burning his fingers.

Now the hat was much too hot to handle. Following his own kind of disastrous logic, Earl popped a pillowcase over the hat, carried it down to the kitchen, and put it in the refrigerator.

17

A Dark Tunnel

In Deep Magic Space, Lulu was sitting where she had fallen, trying not to panic, trying not to cry, and wondering what to do next, when she felt a cool breeze. She crawled toward it and found herself inside a cave every bit as dark as the forest. For a moment she just sat there and let the cool air wash over her. Then, very carefully, she stood up. Remembering what Ben and Laura Lee had told her, she started to walk deeper into the cave, down a long tunnel. Having a direction to go in calmed her, but it was very cold in the tunnel, and Lulu shivered. She wondered what had happened to Ben. Maybe he was somewhere in the tunnel too.

"Ben!" she called. She heard only the echo of her own voice.

She thought about Laura Lee. Where was she now?

Most of all, Lulu worried about Hereboy. Would she ever find him?

"Hereboy!" she called. To her surprise a faint bark answered her call.

"Hereboy!" she called again.

There it was. A definite bark. Lulu kept walking and calling for Hereboy as his bark grew louder and louder.

18

Sneaky Sister

Earl Zopton sat down at the kitchen table with a piece of paper and a pencil. He was waiting for the hat to cool off. Remembering the awful ant experience, he realized that he actually had come up with the right magic words. But which combination of words had they been? He thought he would write down every word in every possible combination he could remember. It wouldn't matter which words were the right ones if he said *all* the words. But he knew better than to say *any* words out loud until he was ready to use the hat again.

Earl never heard his sister come up behind him.

"What's this?" she said as she grabbed the paper off the table and started to read.

"Watza Leafy Waggin Doogie. Thatza Leapin Juicy Doozie. Zatza Leopard Whatta Poodle . . ."

"Stop!" cried Earl, trying to grab the paper.

But it was too late.

"Zatza Lepus Wagra Doozie," read Zoe. "This is gobbledegook!"

She laughed as she dropped the paper back on the table. Then Zoe Zopton opened the refrigerator door to get a drink.

19

The Head Speaks

In Deep Magic Space, Lulu turned a corner and the lights came on. As her eyes adjusted, she saw that she was in a dungeonlike room lit by hundreds of candles. The candles seemed to warm the room.

Lulu noticed that there was a table in a darker corner. On the table there was a plate, and on the plate there was a head. The head spoke:

"WHAT HAVE YOU DONE TO THE WEATHER?" it demanded.

Lulu gasped.

Then she remembered Laura Lee in the box and Ben in the trunk.

"I suppose you want me to find the rest of you," she said.

"No! No! No!" shouted the head angrily, and it disappeared through a hole in the table. When the head reappeared it was attached to the body of a boy several years older than Lulu.

"It's just a trick, done with mirrors . . . no real magic," he said. "But I'm incredibly good at tricks. Here's one you'll like."

The boy turned his back to Lulu. When he whirled around to face her again, he was holding a small brown dog.

"Hereboy!" cried Lulu. "That's my dog!"

"Yes," the boy agreed. But he held on tight to the little dog. "I was hoping you'd come after him. Now I have something that belongs to you. And you have something that belongs to me. I propose a trade."

"How could I possibly have something of yours?" asked Lulu. "I've never seen you before in my life!"

"Actually, you have. But it's been a long time," the boy told her. "My name is Langston Caste . . . Langston Caste *Junior*. And you are my sister."

20

The Trick's on Earl

Zoe Zopton's mouth fell open.

From top to bottom, and side to side, the refrigerator was filled with gerbils. Cold gerbils.

A sound that wasn't quite a word came from Zoe's mouth. She said, "WHAYAHINNNNNNGAH!"

Out onto the kitchen floor poured the shivering rodents, along with the milk, orange juice, eggs, and Lulu's hat.

"WHAH! WHAH! WHAH!" shrieked Zoe as a herd of gerbils raced between her legs.

Earl's first thought was that he had finally played a great trick on his sister.

His second thought was that his mother would be home soon.

"I'm telling!" cried Zoe, finding her voice at last. She raced out the door.

Earl was panicked.

Gotta get the gerbils out of the kitchen! he thought. He opened the door and the gerbils were happy to escape into the warm sun. That was the easy part.

Whenever possible, Earl liked to avoid work. But this was an extreme situation. So Earl got out the mop and went to work on the milky, eggy, juicy mess. Earl had never worked so hard on anything before in his life. In other circumstances, his mother would have been proud of him. The refrigerator and the kitchen floor were spotless when Ernestine Zopton stomped through the door with Zoe right behind. She stopped in her tracks and gave Zoe an angry look.

"Where are the rats?" she said. "You said there were rats! You said the kitchen was a mess. Are you trying to get your brother in trouble?"

Earl flashed an innocent smile at his sister, but his mother continued: "Earl's already in enough trouble. I see he's got that hat again."

Now it was Zoe's turn to smile knowingly at her brother.

"I'm just worried about Earl," she said. "I think he's gone crazy."

She pointed to the paper still lying on the kitchen table.

Oh no! thought Earl. "Don't read it, Mama!" he shouted.

Which was not the right thing to say to Ernestine Zopton. She immediately picked up the paper and started to read.

Earl grabbed the hat and ran down the hall. He had to get it away before more gerbils or ants or anything else poured out. But as Earl raced up the stairs to his room, the hat was already spitting out juicy pink gobs of Palooka bubble gum, unmistakably Earl's favorite brand.

"Come back here, Earl!" shouted his mother. She started up the stairs after him. But she didn't get far. With every step Ernestine Zopton's size twelve shoes ground six or seven sticky blobs of gum into the carpet. Earl's favorite trick was about to get him into even more trouble.

21

A Brother in Deep Magic Space?

Lulu didn't see Ben and Laura Lee emerge from the tunnel. She was staring at a locket Junior wore on a chain around his neck. It was identical to her own. And his eyes. Pale blue, like water. Junior was talking.

"I've been waiting for you," he said. "So much unexplained activity this summer. Rabbits, rodents, and reptiles coming and going. Visits by the same little brown dog. I thought it might be you — at last — playing with the magic hat. It's my hat, you know."

Lulu was spellbound. First the locket, and now this boy seemed to know about the magic hat.

Junior continued: "In our family only one person in each generation is born with real magic. Our father is the great

ONE of his generation. When I was born, he created a hat with magical powers. He said it would remain an ordinary top hat until one touch from the next magician unlocked its magic. He was sure that the next magician would be me, and that the hat would be mine when I was old enough. Then you were born . . . and what happened was entirely your fault!"

"I don't understand," said Lulu. "What happened and why was it my fault?"

But Junior said, "Business first. I'll give you your dog if you give me the hat."

Lulu realized then that Hereboy was nowhere in sight.

"If I had the hat, I'd give it to you," she said. "But I don't have it, and I don't know how to go back and get it."

"All you need are the right magic words," said Junior, suddenly helpful. He snapped his fingers and a small gold book appeared in his hand. It had a lock and looked very much like a diary. "Just look in the book," he said.

"Why don't you look in the book yourself?" asked Lulu.

"I can't," he said. "You're the only one who has the key."

"I don't have the key!" Lulu snapped.

But Junior was looking at Lulu's open locket.

"Yes, you do," he said.

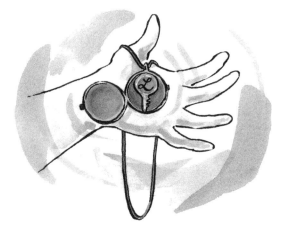

22

Earl Considers His Day

Earl Zopton stood at the top of the stairs. He looked down at the bubble gum minefield that separated him from his angry mother.

"It wasn't me," he whined. "It was the hat."

"The hat," said his mother. "The hat chewed all this bubble gum. This disgusting pink bubble gum that is on the stairs and on my shoes . . . Give me that hat!" she commanded. "I'll make sure it doesn't cause any more trouble."

Her words came out in a low, menacing growl. Every dog in the neighborhood heard it and looked for a place to hide. So did Earl.

It was then that Earl did a quick summary of his day. He had been infested with ants and sprayed with a hose, he'd burned his fingers and had to clean up the biggest mess he'd ever seen, and now he was in more trouble than he could even imagine. Earl Zopton tiptoed down the stairs between gobs of bubble gum and gave his mother the hat.

23

The Key to Magic

Junior gave Lulu the small gold book. It wasn't even as big as her hand. She took the key from her locket and tried it in the lock. The book fell open instantly. But before she could take a look, Junior grabbed it back. He riffled through the pages, then a strange expression came over his face. Junior tossed the book aside and sat down.

"There's nothing in it," he said. "Nothing but blank pages."

Lulu picked up the book and opened it to the title page. At first glance, it was indeed blank. Then words began to form on the page.

"The Key to Magic," she read. "Secrets from Deep Magic Space."

Junior looked up in amazement, and Lulu couldn't resist giving him a triumphant look.

"Get the hat," said Junior. "I promise you'll get your dog back."

"Don't trust him," said Laura Lee.

Lulu didn't. But Hereboy was much more important to her than a hat, even a magic hat.

"I've got to give the hat to him," she said. "Maybe it won't be magic for him."

Lulu looked in the Table of Contents. Under HAT she read:

Basic Use
To Activate Magic
To Send
To Retrieve
To Self-Transport
To Transport Others
To Turn Off Magic
Problem-Solving

Turning to the right page, she found the words and spoke them.

"Karma Kasaka Reven Isto!"

24

The Shortest Chapter

Ernestine Zopton was holding the hat in both hands when she disappeared.

Earl blinked. His mother was gone.

25

Surprise!

In Deep Magic Space, Lulu, Ben, Laura Lee, and Junior couldn't believe their eyes. The magic words had worked. There indeed was the hat, but it was being held by an incredibly large, angry woman. It was Earl Zopton's mother.

Another person might have been stunned into silence by this extraordinary occurrence. Not Ernestine Zopton.

"Where am I and who are you?" she demanded.

"I'll take that," said Junior, snatching the hat. "But you were not part of the bargain," he added, staring rudely at Earl's mother.

Junior did not know Ernestine Zopton. She grabbed him by the ear.

"Where are your parents?" she bellowed, almost lifting him off the ground.

"Yeeouch!" Junior cried out in pain, and he dropped the hat.

Lulu reacted without thinking.

"Stop!" she said to the angry woman. She was astonished to see the woman freeze where she stood, instantly as stiff as a statue, her fingers still firmly attached to Junior's ear.

"Did I do that?" Lulu said. "I'm not wearing the hat."

"Make her let go!" cried Junior.

"Where's my dog?" said Lulu.

Junior's toes barely touched the ground, and the pain in his ear was excruciating. Frantically he pointed to the plate on the table. "Push it!" he gasped. "Push it down!"

Lulu pushed the plate down, and Hereboy leaped out from the hidden compartment beneath the table.

Knowing that this might be her only chance to get some answers from her brother, Lulu quickly asked, "What was my fault and why do I have your hat?"

Junior could feel his ear growing dangerously numb. He started to talk.

"Eleven years ago I sneaked into Father's studio and took down the hat. It was supposed to be mine, and I couldn't wait to unlock its powers. I tried to make the hat do something magic. But nothing happened. 'Dumb hat!' I said just as you came toddling in. The human echo. 'Dumb hat,' you said. You were such a pain, learning to talk, repeating everything you heard. 'Lulu get lost!' I yelled. You picked up the hat, and of course you repeated what I had just said."

Lulu looked blankly at Junior.

"Don't you understand?" Junior shouted. "YOU were the ONE. YOU touched the hat and unlocked the magic. You said, 'Lulu get lost,' and you did. You really got lost! You and the hat disappeared completely. No one could find you. Father and Mother looked everywhere for you. New York, Paris, Rome, London."

"I was in New Jersey," Lulu told him.

Junior looked so sad that Lulu almost felt sorry for him.

"It's not fair," he said.

"Lulu," said Ben, "if you have real magic, can you get us all out of here?"

Lulu looked in her little gold book for the words that would transport them back to Indiana. When she had memorized them, she put the book in her hat and the hat on her head. She cradled Hereboy in the crook of her arm.

"You've got to get home too," she said to the frozen lady. Ernestine Zopton remained motionless. She did not react

when Lulu took her hand from Junior's ear and held it in her own. Junior jumped away and massaged his red ear.

"Everybody hold hands so we're all connected," Lulu said.

Laura Lee took Ernestine Zopton's other hand, and Ben grabbed Laura Lee's hand.

Lulu looked at her brother standing defiantly apart from them. She didn't like him very much, but she felt a connection to him that couldn't be ignored. And there was so much he could tell her, if only he would.

"Junior," she said. "Come with us. Please."

Then she had an inspiration.

"You can work with my Uncle Jerry. You can all work in Jerry's Traveling Magic Show!"

Junior made no move to join them.

"Last chance," said Lulu, and she started to say the magic words. As the last syllable slipped past her lips, Junior lunged for Ben's outstretched hand.

26

Home Again

Earl Zopton was sitting at the foot of the stairs when his mother, four strangers, and a dog appeared. His mother stared into space and did not move until one of the strangers spoke to her. Then she blinked her eyes and her mouth fell open.

"Excuse us," said Lulu. "We're late for the show." The strangers and the dog left by the front door without further explanation.

Earl looked at his mother, and his mother looked at him.

"It was the hat!" they both said at the same time.

Epilogue

Lulu made it back in time for the next performance. After the show she told Jerry her amazing story. Of course her uncle had heard of the great Langston Caste. The total number of True Magic Families in the world was unknown, but Jerry had always suspected that Langston Caste had the gift. Unfortunately he confirmed what Ben had feared. Langston Caste's plane had disappeared while flying over an area known as the Bermuda Triangle. He and his wife were presumed dead. Lulu felt that she had found her birth parents and lost them on the same day. Still, her family had grown. There was, after all, Junior.

Junior joined Lulu and Jerry in the Traveling Magic Show, but Lulu made sure that he never got his hands on the hat. She knew that it was her hat. It had been folded up, lying in the bottom of Jerry's old costume trunk all those years, waiting for Lulu to reclaim it and discover her powers. Having seen those powers at work, Junior was inclined to behave. In the fall, he stayed with Uncle Jerry and they continued to travel around the country and abroad. Junior had great success, even without real magic. He was, as he had boasted, unsurpassed when it came to sleight of hand. He also had his father's imagination and created many new tricks for the act. With success his anger seemed to fade, and after a while even Hereboy stopped growling at him.

Laura Lee decided to form her own traveling magic show. Ben went with her to be her assistant.

Lulu went back to school in September. She realized that her magic powers had been growing ever since she first pulled the hat out of Jerry's trunk. But, as Jerry had said, uncontrolled magic was a dangerous thing, and she knew she still had a lot to learn. Every night, after she had finished her homework, she could always be found curled up with her dog and a good book. A very special book.